World's Best "True" Ghost Stories

C. B. COLBY

Sterling Publishing Co., Inc.   New York

Library of Congress Cataloging-in-Publication Data

Colby, C.B. (Carroll B.)
  The world's best "true" ghost stories / by C.B. Colby.
      p.   cm.
  Includes index.
  ISBN 0-8069-6876-1
  1. Ghosts—Juvenile literature.   I. Title.
BF1461.C67   1988
133.1—dc19   88-11703
                                                    CIP
                                                     AC

The material in this book has been
excepted from the following books:
Strangely Enough! copyright © 1959
by C.B. Colby and *The Weirdest
People in the World,* copyright © 1973,
1965 by C.B. Colby,
both published by Sterling Publishing Co., Inc.
This edition published in 1988 by Sterling Publishing Co., Inc.
387 Park Avenue South, New York, N.Y. 10016
Distributed in Canada by Sterling Publishing
% Canadian Manda Group, P.O. Box 920, Station U
Toronto, Ontario, Canada M8Z 5P9
Distributed in Great Britain and Europe by Cassell PLC
Artillery House, Artillery Row, London SWIP IRT, England
Distributed in Australia by Capricorn Ltd.
P.O. Box 665, Lane Cove, NSW 2066
Manufactured in the United States of America
Sterling ISBN 0-8069-6898-2 (pbk.)

Contents

To the Reader

A good yarn, an offbeat tale, a bloodcurdling ghost story—they need no explanation or excuse for the telling! We are presenting them solely for your entertainment, your wonderment and perhaps for a few enjoyable chills. Perhaps you have already encountered a few of these stories in local versions, or perhaps you are actually the person to whom "it" happened!

All of the accounts in this book have, at one time or another, been passed off as "true." The only ones I can vouch for are those that I experienced personally, and sometimes I wonder about even those. The others are classics of their kind that have been told and retold—and who shall say they never happened? I think it's better to be like the person who said, "I don't believe in ghosts—but I'm afraid of them!" than never to have enjoyed a bit of spine-tingling at a personal encounter with the unknown.

As long as there are events that seem supernatural and cannot be explained away by serious and logical means—as long as there is a single, chilling chance that there might be such things, we will at least have fine yarns to tell and listen to! May there always be at least one more!

1. STRANGE!

Could these weird tales possibly be true? The people who told them assured us that they were. What do you think?

The Light in the Window

On a train travelling west through Canada one night, some of us were sitting up pretty late telling yarns. One fellow told this story.

A friend of his who lived in Ontario became fascinated with an old painting he saw in a dingy little store. The picture was of a dramatic-looking castle on a hilltop. The scene was dark and gloomy and every window in the castle was dark except for a small one high in a stone tower. The man wondered why anyone would paint a castle with a light in just one window. Was there a story behind it? He bought the painting and hung it in his home, but all the storekeeper could tell him was that it depicted a castle in Scotland. There was neither signature nor date.

One day, as he was cleaning the painting, he found a few Latin words in a corner. He asked a friend to translate the words, and learned that they meant "every century it will be dark." This inscription made little sense to him, and he forgot about it. The painting hung in the man's home for many years, and friends enjoyed speculating about why the window was lighted. It was quite a conversation piece.

One evening the owner of the painting was telling some guests about how he had acquired it and answering questions about its background and meaning. The guests wanted to see this unusual and mysterious piece of art, so they all trooped into the hall where it hung. Imagine their astonishment and the consternation of their host when they saw that, on the painting, the window in the tower was dark!

Examining the painting closely, they were astonished to see that the black paint on the once light yellow window was as old and cracked as the paint on the rest of the picture. There were no signs that it had ever been different, let alone bright yellow.

After the guests had gone, the embarrassed host unsuccessfully tried to find a solution to the puzzle. The next morning he returned to the painting and felt his skin crawl! The window in the tower was lighted! Then he thought of the Latin inscription, "every century it will be dark." He made a note of the date and began a serious search into Scottish history. Eventually these facts were uncovered. The castle had been the home of an evil character who had two sons. He hated the elder son and kept him locked in the tower while his younger son enjoyed all the wealth and pleasures he could give him. Exactly five hundred years before the night when the painted window had gone dark, the imprisoned elder son had died in the little room high in the tower.

The Sound of the Drip

This eerie encounter is said to have taken place around West Chazy in New York State.

Not long ago a local resident, deciding to go fishing in a nearby pond, dug himself some worms, cut himself a nice pole, and, taking his dog, clambered into an old flat-bottomed boat for a quiet afternoon.

The dog curled up in the bottom of the boat and fell asleep almost as soon as the man had baited his hook and tossed it over. The fish just weren't biting. The man rowed from one spot to another, trying first here and then there along the shore. It was almost as though all of the fish in the pond had been caught or were in hiding.

Finally the man decided to try his luck in the middle of the little lake, where the water was deepest. The moment he anchored there, the dog, who had been sound asleep all the time so far, woke with a start and began to whine and tremble. The man spoke sharply to him, telling him to be quiet and to lie down. The dog obeyed, but he kept whining softly and trembling violently.

Hardly had the man dropped his hook to the bottom when he felt a tug. He began to pull on the line, but it seemed to hold fast to the bottom. At this point, the dog jumped to his feet and began to bark viciously, showing his teeth and peering over the side of the boat, rocking it sharply. The man, struggling with the line, gave the dog a blow with one of the oars, which sent him into the other end of the boat, where he cringed, whimpering.

Once more the man heaved his stout pole. Slowly, it came to the surface—whatever it was. Tangled on the end of the line was a great clump of what looked like human hair. Shining in it was a bright golden barrette. As the man brought the object over the side of the boat, the dog let out a howl of terror and plunged into the lake, heading for shore. He soon made it and vanished into the woods.

The man was amazed at the actions of the dog, but nevertheless decided to take the hair home and give the barrette to his wife. She could use it, he thought, to hold her hair back. The barrette was so entangled that they would have to hang the hair before the fire to dry out to make removal easier. His wife, though horrified at the idea, coveted the bright barrette and so consented.

Long after the strands of hair were dry the sound of dripping still could be heard. It went on all evening. Then, at the stroke of twelve, a woman's voice came from the hanging strands. It told of her murder and how her body could be recovered. Then the voice faded away and was heard no more. The man and his wife couldn't believe what they'd heard and decided to keep it to themselves for the time being, particularly so that the wife could keep the valuable barrette.

However, the dripping sound continued. It went on all night and all the next day, and the day after that. Finally, they could stand it no longer and reported their find to the authorities. Police dredged the lake and recovered the body, which was identified by the golden barrette.

The dog never returned.

The Man and the Glove

While sight-seeing in Scotland, a young American woman joined a group that was visiting an island where a crumbling castle had recently been opened to the public. As they approached the castle, the young lady noticed that a huge cloud overhead looked like a pair of gauntlet gloves. She called it to the attention of the others in the party, but thought no more about it. The unusual cloud formation soon faded away.

Later that day a sudden and violent storm came up. Because the trip back to the mainland was too rough for their small boat, the sight-seers were forced to spend the night at the castle. The young American was given a room in one of the towers. She went to bed quite thrilled at the opportunity to spend the night there.

Awakening during the night, she was surprised to see a pair of white gauntlets on the floor by her bed. The gloves were surrounded by a halo of light that illuminated a crest embroidered in red silk. As the bewildered woman raised her eyes from the strange sight, she was even more startled to see a tall, dark young man looking at her from the shadows beyond the gloves. At her gasp of terror, both the glowing gloves and the young man vanished.

Perhaps, she thought, it had been a dream, inspired by the gauntlet-shaped cloud she had seen earlier. She didn't mention her ghostly visitor to anyone.

Several years passed. In New York, she met a young Scotsman and married him. Shortly after their honeymoon, he received word that a maiden aunt had died in New England, and the newlyweds had to go there to close the house. It was very run down and dilapidated, with hardly a sign that it had been lived in. The young bride occupied herself by poking about the attic. There in an old trunk, neatly wrapped in a bit of tartan, was a pair of white gauntlets, exactly the same as those she had seen in the castle years before.

She hurried downstairs in excitement to show them to her husband and tell him about the strange coincidence. When she held them out to him, he turned deathly pale. "So, my dear," he said, "you were the girl in the bed that night!" Then he vanished—for the second time! His bride fainted, and when she came to, she was alone. Questioning the neighbors later, she was told that no one had lived in the old house for a hundred years. She never saw her husband again.

The Spell on the Mirror

In the War Memorial Hospital at Sault Ste. Marie, Michigan, Jefferey Derosier was close to death. He knew he was critically ill, and so did the three other patients who shared the small ward.

One afternoon Derosier asked the nurse to hand him the small mirror from the enamel table beside his bed. The nurse gave him the mirror, which was just a plain piece of silvered glass without a frame or handle.

A moment later he threw it back upon the bedside table and cried hysterically, "I'm dying!" The other patients, watching him, were stunned. He spoke again in a low, dull voice. "You won't be able to pick up that mirror," he said. Then he died.

After his body had been removed, one of the other patients casually tried to pick up the mirror. He couldn't budge it from where it lay on the white table. Baffled, he asked the nurse to pick it up, but she couldn't move it either.

A doctor was called and he too tried to lift the mirror from its place. It would not move. Soon word of the "haunted" mirror spread throughout the hospital. Nurses, interns and curious patients all tried to move the little mirror from where the dying man had thrown it. No one succeeded. All day the mirror defied every attempt to move it. Even when a nurse tried to pry it loose with an ice pick, it remained sealed to the table top.

Then another nurse tried to work her fingernail under the edge of the little piece of glass. As if at that moment the spell was broken, the mirror flew several feet into the air and fell to the floor unbroken. At last it had moved.

Trying to find a reason for the mirror sticking to the table as long as it had, some of the witnesses attempted to make it stick again. But they couldn't do it. There was no adhesive on the back of the piece of silvered glass and anyone could now pick it up easily from the dry table top. They wet the surface in an attempt to create suction so that the mirror would stick once more, but the spell was broken. Later the mirror was cracked, perhaps on purpose, and thrown away. There was never any explanation of the spell cast by Jefferey Derosier's dying words.

The Iron Tomahawk

This weird incident took place recently in northern Vermont, near the Canadian line, and its authenticity was sworn to by the farmer to whom it happened. This man had a dream.

According to his story, when he was a very young boy in 1910, he was greatly intrigued by tales of the Indians who had once lived near his home. Every corner of the woods had some historic spot and some accompanying legend about the deeds of daring and terror that had taken place there.

The farmer's boyhood excitement and interest was rekindled one day 30 years later when he found an old iron tomahawk in a gravel pit near where he used to play after school. He carved a crude handle out of wood and attached it to the tomahawk, and this became his most treasured possession. One day he "lost" it. How it came to be lost is a weird story. How it was found again is even more unbelievable.

One night the farmer dreamed he was a small boy again, coming home from school. Suddenly an Indian was chasing him, threatening him, following him all the way. When he got home, his parents were out, and he had to face the Indian alone. To save his life he grabbed the old tomahawk and struck the Indian a great blow on the head, killing him instantly and just in time.

In the dream he dragged the savage out into the pasture and buried him so that his parents would not find the body in the house. The dream was so real and so vivid that the next day the farmer rather sheepishly went to the pasture to see if it just could have been true. Of course, there was no sign of any grave or digging, and he felt much relieved. When asked where he had been, he laughingly told his grown children about his dream, and they kidded him about it for long afterwards.

Strangely enough, he could not find his prized tomahawk from that night on, no matter where he looked for it.

Just a few years ago, the farmer happened to cross that same corner of the pasture and to his astonishment noticed a shallow depression in the sod exactly where he had dreamed he had buried the Indian. He was startled and a bit disturbed, but put it aside as a natural sinking of the land. Still he could not get it out of his mind.

For weeks he fought off an urge to dig at that spot. Finally, more in jest than in expectation, he got a spade and went to work, hoping no one would see him. He was glad no one had, for a few feet down he came across a skeleton. In the skull was buried an iron tomahawk with a crude wooden handle. *It was the handle he had whittled himself.*

According to the farmer, he filled in the hole and to this day he never revealed the spot to anyone. Who could blame him?

2. OFF THE TIME TRACK?

Probably all of us, at one time or other, have encountered something that seemed out of sync. It might be a vision of something that didn't belong—perhaps something in the wrong place at the wrong time. Here are a few curious tales of things that may have been off the time track.

Tunnel to the Past

This fantastic incident is rumored to have occurred recently on a mountainside "somewhere out West." The person who reported it to me was a skeptic from New Mexico who didn't believe it actually happened. But he had been assured it was true by the person who told it to him. And, he found it intriguing. . . .

It seems that an amateur mineral collector was on a trip West, and he enjoyed exploring old mine shafts or tunnels he spotted from the highway. His wife was used to these side trips. She usually knitted in their car while he hunted for rocks for his collection.

On one trip, he spotted a dark opening in the side of a high ridge. Stopping the car, he took his collecting bag and geologist's hammer, and started off. He entered the cave and was soon in the gloom of a walk-in tunnel, apparently an old mine shaft. The roof seemed solid, and there seemed to be no snakes about; so cautiously he walked deeper into the shaft. After some distance, he noticed light up ahead. He hurried on, surprised that there should be another entrance so soon.

Moving forward, he came to a fork in the tunnel. One passage was dark and the other filled with an odd light from up ahead. Having no flashlight with him, he decided to follow the lighter corridor. He turned left into one of the most astonishing experiences a rock hound ever had. As the tunnel grew lighter, he saw a small opening before him about two feet wide and a foot high. He got to his knees and looked into it and saw a wide valley stretched out below.

Then he gaped. In the center of this valley was a wagon train in a defensive circle. From one side a great horde of mounted Indians was attacking, waving bows and arrows and spears and whooping loudly enough to make his blood run cold.

Of course, he thought he was viewing a set for a TV show or a movie and, after recovering from his initial shock, watched with disinterested fascination. But the slaughter became so realistic and the screams of the wounded so fearful that his interest soon turned to horror and then panic. He finally tore his eyes away from the sight and with his fingers in his ears raced back through the tunnel. He burst out of the shaft just as his wife was coming to find him.

He told her what he had seen, and she, in equal panic, said he had been gone over an hour and she had become worried. She had brought a flashlight with her. Together they went back into the tunnel. They could find no fork in the corridor, only a dead end a few feet inside the opening. The fork just wasn't there.

Later, when they described the incident, local residents seemed quite excited, for in the valley just behind the ridge where the tunnel was, an entire wagon train of pioneers had been massacred by Indians many years before. Perhaps through the now-vanished tunnel to the past he had witnessed a reenactment of the actual scene. Perhaps it was just as well he came back to modern times when he did. A little longer might have been too late.

The Phantom Schooner

It happened years ago in the Caribbean, where I was on a patrol cruiser trying to apprehend some smugglers.

The little cruiser was hidden in a tiny palm-ringed cove one night, awaiting the appearance of a small schooner that was known to be in operation in the area. The only light came from the stars and a blinker buoy at sea beyond the entrance to the cove. The moon was down, but by the light of the stars we could distinguish between sea and sky and shore line. We watched and waited.

An hour or so past midnight, one of the crew spotted the dark sails of a small sailboat appearing above the beach by the cove entrance. Soon the silhouette of the little boat, silent and dark, passed in front of us. It blotted out the blinking light from the buoy and disappeared behind the point of land to the right of the cove. It might be our quarry.

We pulled up the anchor, started the engines and moved silently out of the cove, turning south along the coast and keeping close to shore. Ahead of us, also close to shore, we could faintly see the outline of the schooner beating along under a stiff onshore breeze.

As we gained on the boat ahead we prepared for what might turn out to be more than just routine checking of a vessel without legal lights. A belt of ammunition was fed into the machine gun on our bow. Sidearms and rifles were passed up from the gunlockers below. The spray jacket was removed from the big searchlight atop the cabin roof.

Our usual procedure was to come up a bit to the windward and astern of a suspicious craft, snap on the powerful beam and then close in for action, depending upon what the searchlight revealed. A small schooner without running lights beating close to shore late at night could mean most anything: a careless skipper with a fine disregard for regulations, a forgetful native crew coming home from a celebration in one of the small villages—or it might be the schooner we were after.

We drew close astern of the silhouetted schooner, swung to windward of it so that our boat would cut the wind and slow the boat ahead, and snapped on our big beam. There was absolutely nothing there!

We swung our huge beam around the area, even up and down, but our quarry had vanished. What had we seen, or what had we thought we had seen?

Hitchhiker to Montgomery

Driving toward Montgomery, Alabama, late one evening, two businessmen planned to spend the night in a small town, on the way. They were making good time through some low country where the road was a few feet above the surrounding land. Their headlights picked up a figure far ahead. As they drew nearer, they discovered that it was a little old lady walking briskly along the side of the road. Slowing down to speak to her, they saw that she wore a pale lavender dress, freshly pressed and sparkling clean. Her hair was neatly done and she turned a smiling face to them. She seemed completely untroubled about walking down a lonely highway in the middle of the night.

When the men asked what she was doing on the road at that time of night, she laughingly explained that she had started out to visit her daughter and grandchildren in Montgomery. She had hoped, she said, to get a ride for at least part of the way, but no one had offered her a lift; so she had just kept on walking.

The two men said they would give her a lift as far as the next town, a two-hour drive, and she was delighted to accept. She sat in the back seat and, as they drove through the night, talked about her daughter and three grandchildren—their names, where they lived, the children's school—the usual small talk among strangers. When the subject was exhausted, the men eventually became engrossed in business conversation and forgot about the passenger behind them.

When they reached their destination they stopped to let the elderly lady out. She was gone. Panic-stricken to think that she might have fallen out along the way, they headed back in search of her. But they found no signs of their passenger, even though they retraced their route to where they had picked her up, and saw her tiny footprints in the shoulder of the road where she had first talked to them.

Dismayed and mystified, they drove on to Montgomery and found her daughter's name and number in the local phone book. They felt they had to tell her about what appeared to be a terrible accident. After listening to their story in bewilderment, the younger woman pointed to three photos on the mantel. Could they identify their passenger? They did, and she agreed that it was her mother. Without a doubt, they had talked to her. They went on to describe her dress, and the woman burst into tears. That was the dress, she said, her mother had worn when she last saw her.

"When was that?" they asked. The woman replied between sobs, "When she was buried, just three years ago today!"

The Haunted Cabin

Near an eastern entrance to Yellowstone Park in Wyoming, there used to be a crude log shack known as the Haunted Cabin. Here's how it came by that name.

The cabin had long been deserted when one night, many years ago, a forest ranger camped in it. Just as he managed to fall asleep, he was awakened by a loud pawing and snorting just outside in the snow. It sounded as though some other ranger had ridden up on his horse and was about to enter.

He lay there for several minutes while the noises continued. But no other ranger came to pound on the door. Finally he began to feel uneasy and, taking his gun, crept to the door and threw it open. There was no one there, neither man nor horse.

Lighting a lantern he circled the cabin, but could find no tracks. Baffled, he went back to bed. Presently the snorting and pawing began again. Again he rose and searched the area around the cabin clearing, but to no avail.

The rest of his night was spent tossing and turning, trying to shut out the loud sounds from outside. The next morning he made still another search, found nothing, and left, glad to be away from the place.

Several other campers and hunters stayed at this cabin during the following months, and all sooner or later reported the same snorting and pawing sounds outside, although none of them had heard any rumors about a phantom horse and rider at the cabin.

Finally one camper, after a restless night, decided to investigate further. He researched the annals of the Yellowstone area in local libraries and came up with a newspaper account which may or may not explain the weird incident, but which was intriguing.

He learned that many years before the first ranger reported the pawing sounds, a drunken cowboy had spent an extremely cold winter night in the cabin. He had tied his horse to the tree by the door and stumbled inside to sleep a frigid eight hours wrapped in his blankets. The horse, left uncovered and freezing outside, pawed and snorted to get free. The next morning the cowboy found his horse dead in the snow.

Perhaps the horse's ghost was still trying to get free from that tree. Or perhaps it was just coincidence that all those who stayed in the cabin seemed to hear the same sounds in the night. The incidents remain strange and baffling. . . .

3. GHOSTLY ANIMALS

Many people believe that animals, particularly dogs, can sense the presence of ghosts or other supernatural beings when mere humans are not aware of them. Perhaps it is true. Certainly, there are many tales about animals who show great fear or love toward someone or something no one else can see. But stories of animal ghosts or animals who are bewitched are a bit less common. Here are a few stories of both kinds.

Night Ride

This story was told by an old doctor who lived a hermit's life in a small New England village. It happened when he was a young boy, but he told it and retold it in exactly the same way until his death.

When the doctor was fifteen years old, his father had a bay colt which he let his son ride. One evening the boy started riding to a nearby town. On the way he had to pass a cottage where a woman by the name of Dolly Spokesfield lived. She was rumored to have unusual powers, skill in the black arts and the ability to turn herself into almost anything she wished. She was, it was whispered, a genuine witch of the inner circle—certainly a person to be avoided by anyone out at night alone.

As the lad approached Dolly Spokesfield's cottage he kept to the middle of the road and urged the colt to a faster trot. But his precautions were in vain.

As the colt and rider came abreast of the cottage, a coal black cat suddenly leaped out of the darkness and landed on the colt's neck. The frightened horse stopped short, almost throwing the boy over his head. The boy tried desperately to get rid of the cat and urged his mount on, beating him with his whip, but the cat held on and the colt refused to move with the black cat hissing upon his neck.

The boy was afraid to leave his horse and run, and in panic he dismounted and began to beat the cat with the whip, holding the colt by the bridle rein as he reared and plunged, trying to shake off the cat.

At last the boy dislodged the cat and he hurriedly rode home. The poor colt was bruised and clawed by the cat, and apparently exhausted by his ordeal. So injured and frightened was he that the boy was afraid the animal would die before morning. He turned him loose in the barn instead of putting him in the stall, and went to bed trembling and fearful that the colt wouldn't last the night.

At dawn, the boy hurried to the barn to inspect the battered and clawed animal. To his amazement, the young horse was in perfect condition. He showed no sign of exhaustion, and nowhere on his body could the boy find a trace of bruises from the whip, a claw mark or a single reminder of the frantic events of the previous night.

The story had an even stranger ending. A neighbor soon stopped by to report that Dolly Spokesfield had just been found almost dead, her body bruised and beaten as though by a whip. And under two of her fingernails were some short bay hairs, such as you'd find, perhaps, on the neck of a young colt ridden by a frightened boy alone in the night.

The Dream Dog

Retired Colonel Elmer G. Parker, of Riverdale, New York, had a most unusual dream some years ago. The dream and its aftermath baffled the Colonel. Maybe it will baffle you, too.

Colonel Parker had the dream on the night of a snowstorm. Unable to sleep, he had come down to the living room in his robe and slippers, poked up the logs in the fireplace, and settled down on a couch in front of the fire. A few years before, when his beloved Irish setter, Laddie, was alive, he liked sleeping on that same couch, but at no time during the evening had the Colonel thought of the dog.

Presently Colonel Parker fell asleep and dreamed vividly. The dog came to him and touched his knee, first with his nose and then with his paw, as a sign he wished to go out. The gentleman did not remember dreaming that he got on his coat and hat, but simply that he took the dog's leash and went out into the snowy street with him.

He dreamed that the dog ran down the steps and across the yard, rubbing his nose in the newly fallen snow, while Parker walked behind him with the leash, having turned him loose to run. For some moments the dog raced about. Then they returned to the house and the Colonel once more lay down on the couch to continue his sleep. They had met no one on the deserted street, or at least they had not in the dream.

About five-thirty in the morning Colonel Parker woke up feeling cold. The fire had gone out. The door to the living room was wide open, not as he had left it. He reached down for his slippers and found them soaking wet. Startled, he hurried to the front door and found the entrance hall was also wet. He looked out the front door onto the stoop and down across the snow-covered yard. There were his slipper prints in the fresh snow, down across the yard and back again, and beside them, both going and coming, were the footprints of a large dog, about the size of those made by an Irish setter.

The Witch Cat of the Catskills

Spook Woods, a strange spot in the Catskill Mountains of New York State, deserved its name. It was said that even dull-witted cattle who wandered into these woods would suddenly rush away in panic at what they had encountered. Certainly horses often balked at taking the road that ran through Spook Woods. The local people usually managed to go through it only in broad daylight, and preferably with company.

A farmhand named Williams, the story goes, had been hired to work on a farm on the other side of the woods from his home. Williams had heard tales of Spook Woods, as who up that way hadn't? But he was a big, rugged and ordinarily fearless man who paid little attention to tales of witches and supernatural happenings.

However, one winter night as he returned home through the woods on foot, he did feel a certain uneasiness. It was only because of the full moon that cast odd shadows along the side of the dirt road, he reassured himself. But as he reached the center of the wooded stretch, he realized that one shadow was hurrying along *ahead* of him. This shadow was more than a trick of moonlight, for it was moving quickly over the snow along the roadside.

As he hurried to pass it, he saw to his astonishment that the shadow was made by two cats who were dragging an obviously dead cat between them. What a strange way for animals to act, he thought, as he quickened his steps. The cats hurried too and kept right up with him. Then, to his increasing horror, one of them called him by name. Startled as he was, he wouldn't—he couldn't—stop. The terrified man began to run, desperately anxious to get out of the woods as fast as possible.

The cats, slowed down by their burden, could not match his speed, but just as he was leaving the thick woods for the open country beyond, one of them screeched in a loud, clear and almost human voice, "Mr. Williams, oh, Mr. Williams, when you get home tell Molly Myers that she can come home now. Old Man Hawkins is dead."

Terribly shaken by his experience, Williams raced home. Once he reached its warm, friendly atmosphere he hesitated to tell anyone about his harrowing experience. Later in the evening, when his family was sitting around the fireplace, he half-jokingly told about it, and finally repeated the odd message.

To everyone's astonishment, the old white cat lying by the hearth sprang to her feet, and without once looking back, leaped up the chimney right over the burning logs and was never seen again. Was that Molly Myers? Had she at last gone home?

The Frightened Dog

Tom grew up in North Carolina, where he, two of his friends and his dog often went hunting in the woods and swamps.

One day they set forth with their guns, planning to be gone only a few hours. Late that afternoon it began to rain very hard. Since they were far from home, they decided to spend the night in an abandoned shack they had stumbled upon, rather than try to find their way home in the dark. The shack was empty except for some rubbish, a few old clothes and a lantern that still had some kerosene in it. Eventually the boys fell asleep on the floor, with the dog curled up beside them, while the rain splattered upon the roof overhead.

During the night the boys were awakened by the dog whining and scratching at the door. He was trembling violently, and the hair on his back was raised as though he were either frightened or angry.

Rather sleepily, one of the boys started for the door to let the pup out. Then he froze in his tracks. From the black woods outside the shack came a weird, startling sound. A combination of whine, low moan, and rising and falling wail, it was like nothing the boys had heard before anywhere. They stared at each other, and reached for their light rifles as the dog raced around the room, barking and whining and showing his teeth. One boy quickly lit the lantern.

The window openings of the shack contained no glass but were covered with mosquito netting. Suddenly the dog hurled himself through one of these openings and ran off into the woods, snarling and barking.

The three boys waited with hearts pounding and .22's clutched in their hands. At last the strange sound faded away in the distance and they heard nothing but the patter of the rain on the tin roof.

A few minutes later the dog leaped back through the broken netting and came toward them, whining and shaking, with his tail tucked between his legs. He was a very frightened white dog. That was the most amazing part of the adventure, for when he had left the shack to run into the woods after the "thing," he had been black!

The White Dove

Many years ago in an Alabama village there lived a man and his wife who were supremely happy together. After years of wedded bliss the wife became very ill, and nothing could be done to save her. On her deathbed she announced to the family and servants that she would return to the garden in the form of a white dove so that she could be with her husband in the place where they had known such true love and happiness. Moments later she died.

Years passed, but no white dove appeared to carry out the dying wife's promise. Eventually the widower fell in love with another woman and decided to marry her and bring her to the big house to live. On the day he carried his new bride between the white pillars and into the house, a white dove came fluttering into the garden and perched upon a white snowball bush by the gate. It uttered long, low moans as though it were heartbroken.

Every afternoon it returned to moan and sigh on the snowball bush. The servants were upset and frightened.

Sure enough, they thought, the first wife's promise had been carried out! Eventually the second wife heard the story and she too became disturbed. Soon people came from the village and from neighboring plantations to stare over the garden wall at the dove on the snowball bush. The new wife grew nervous and ill-tempered and the happy home began to crumble. The husband, frantic, decided upon drastic action. Legend or no legend, he wanted to preserve his new life.

The next afternoon he seized his rifle and slipped from the house, stealthily working his way into the garden, where the dove sat moaning and sobbing on the snowball bush. He raised his rifle and fired. A woman's scream answered the blast of the gun and the dove flew away, its breast reddened with blood.

That night as the husband slept, he died. No one could determine the cause. His widow moved away to escape the tragic memories, and the great house fell into ruins.

The master of the house was buried by the snowball bush. His gravestone, they say, is still there, but there are no visitors. No, there is one. For it is said that every spring when the blossoms of the snowball bush first open, a white dove with a red-splotched breast appears among them, moaning pitifully.

Ghost Dog on the Stair

A ghost dog was seen in 1929, not once but several times, and not only by humans but by dogs as well. One human who saw it was Pierre van Paassen, world-famous author of *Days of Our Years*.

In the spring of that year, van Paassen was living in Bourg-en-Forêt in France. One night he was startled to see a black dog pass him on the stairs of the house in which he was staying. It reached the landing and disappeared. Van Paassen searched the house, but could not find any sign of it. He assumed it must have been a stray that had wandered in and out again.

A few days later he left on a short trip, not thinking much more about the dog on the stairs.

When he returned, however, he found the household greatly upset. During his absence several others had also seen the black dog, and always on the stairs. Van Paassen decided to stake out and watch for the ghostly animal the following night. For corroborating witnesses, he invited a neighbor, Monsieur Grevecoeur, and his young son to join him.

Sure enough, the same black dog appeared at the head of the stairs. Grevecoeur whistled, as he would at any ordinary dog. The dog wagged its tail in friendly fashion. The three men started up the stairs. To their amazement the black animal began to fade and it vanished before they could reach it.

A few evenings later van Paassen stood watch again,

this time accompanied by two police dogs. Once more the ghostly animal appeared and this time came part way down the stairs before it vanished. A moment later the two police dogs were seemingly engaged in a death struggle with an invisible adversary, and presently one of the huge dogs fell to the floor dead. Examination failed to reveal any outward signs of injury.

This was too much for the owner. He called in a priest to advise him. The Abbé de la Roudaire arrived and watched with van Paassen the next night. When the black dog appeared the priest stepped towards it. The beast gave a low growl and faded away once more.

The Abbé at once asked the owner of the house if there was a young girl employed there. The owner admitted that there was, but also wanted to know why the priest had asked. Did the good Abbé think that there might be some connection between the young girl and the mysterious apparition?

The Abbé shrugged his shoulders and said there was sometimes an affinity between young people and some types of mysterious happenings. The girl was dismissed—and the black ghost dog on the stairs was never seen again.

4. PARTYING WITH GHOSTS

Not all ghosts are frightening. Some of them seem to be enjoying themselves, at least for a while. Others are occasionally downright good company. You'll meet a variety of social spirits, in these odd tales. . . .

A Night with the Dead

It happened in the 1890's. A middle-aged couple driving a buggy along a New England road were overtaken by darkness. Not knowing how far away was the next town, they started looking for a place to spend the night. Soon they spotted a light to one side of the road and up a lane through the trees. They turned their tired horse and drove towards it.

The light turned out to be in a small farmhouse on a little hill between two huge elms. The husband rapped on the door, while his wife sat in the buggy.

An aged couple came to the door with a kerosene lamp. When the situation was explained to them, they invited the travellers in for the night. The two couples got along pleasantly, found that they had much in common and, after a warming cup of tea, they all retired. The host refused any payment for the lodgings.

The next morning the travellers rose early to be on their way. So as not to embarrass their host and hostess, they left some silver coins on the table in the hall before they slipped out of the house to hitch up their horse.

Driving to the next town, which proved to be just a couple of miles farther through the woods, they stopped at an inn for breakfast.

Over coffee, they mentioned to the innkeeper where they had stopped the night before and how much they had enjoyed talking with the old couple. The innkeeper looked at them in astonishment. They couldn't have done any such thing, he told them, for he knew the house and the Edmunds who had lived there. The Edmunds had died 20 years before.

The travellers were incredulous. Edmunds was the name the old couple had given them. Their descriptions of the couple tallied with the innkeeper's but the travellers *knew* they had spoken with the Edmunds and drunk tea with them.

"Impossible," scoffed the innkeeper. The Edmunds had been burned to death in a fire that had completely destroyed their home and it had never been rebuilt. The argument grew hot. Finally the travellers insisted on driving the innkeeper back to the farm to prove they had slept there the night before.

Back they went the two miles. There, to their horror, all they found was an empty cellar hole overgrown with weeds and filled with burned timbers and blackened furniture. The couple could not believe their eyes. But then it was the innkeeper's turn to pale. With a cry of terror, the wife pointed a shaky finger at one spot in the charred rubble below them.

On what might have been a hall table, shone a half dollar and two quarters, just the amount the travellers had left in payment that morning while the Edmunds were still "asleep."

Sam Plays the Ghost from South Troy

A ghost in South Troy, New York, was a kindly soul who paid dividends in dollars for decent behavior towards him. His story has been circulating for many years now, and while no one seems to know what happened to the people involved, it goes like this:

Although the old house in South Troy was quite well furnished, it was never occupied for long. The tenants always found some excuse for moving out after a few weeks or even days. They said it was too scary to live in, and all gave the same account as to why. It seems that every midnight a white-bearded old man, tall and thin, came clumping down from the attic and stalked into the parlor, where he stopped in front of some oil paintings and tapped them with his cane or pointed at them. After this he would clump out again and up to his attic. No one could touch him or stop him, but everyone could see him.

It was said that if you stood in front of him he would walk right through you and it felt like a cool breeze blowing in your face. He'd never stop, even if the doors were locked shut before him.

Many tenants, as might be expected, told their stories to Sam, the saloonkeeper at Jefferson and First Streets. Sam never blinked. The landlord was beginning to think he would never rent the place to anyone when he hit on an idea. He offered Sam and two friends of his a hundred dollars each to spend the night there. Sam, the landlord thought, would see no ghost and would soon dispel the fear in South Troy. Sam agreed and took his friends to the house to play pinochle.

But at the stroke of midnight, the old man did clump down again, and Sam saw him, just as he had been described. Without a word he went to the oil paintings, tapped each with his cane, then started back up towards the attic. Sam stood in his way and got walked through, but it didn't perturb him. It seemed to Sam that the old man was rather lonely and unhappy if he went about walking through people without saying hello. He ran around to the front of the old man and gestured towards the pinochle table, offering him a chance to sit in on a few hands. The old man frowned, puzzled, for a few moments. Then he floated over to the table and sat down. He couldn't hold the cards too well, due possibly to fluctuations in his ectoplasm. Occasionally his fingers would become transparent and the cards would fall to the table. He would seem to apologize. Also, Sam reported, he played a rather naïve game of pinochle. Sam debated whether to throw the game to make the old man happy, but he decided against it.

After a half-hour of pinochle the old man was apparently bored. He rose, banged heavily on the oil paintings—one, two, ten times—with his cane, and clumped back up to the attic, nodding politely to Sam, but yawning nevertheless.

After some thought, Sam went to the paintings and took them down. The wallpaper behind them had a fist-size hollow with no plaster behind it. Sam stuck his hand through the paper and pulled out over $50,000 in United States Government Series E War Bonds. He later used them to open a large cocktail lounge on Second and Washington Streets.

The old man continued to be seen, however. It is said he clumps down from the attic even today. His hoard is gone and he carries no cane or pointer, but merely a mournful expression on his face, as if he feels he may have paid too much for a half-hour's entertainment!

Lucky at Cards

It was a cold and stormy night at about the turn of the century. The patrons of the Buxton Inn in Maine were sitting around a roaring fire in the taproom, swapping yarns. Suddenly there was a loud, insistent knocking at the door.

The innkeeper hurried to open it and a young man entered. His rich clothes were trimmed with gold lace and he carried a cape over his arm. He shook the snow from his tall beaver hat, stamped his booted feet and strode to the fireplace.

The others looked up with interest, admiring his elegance, but also noting that his clothes were old-fashioned and a bit strange. Undoubtedly, they thought, he was a traveller from some distant city. One of them offered him a place close to the fire, and suggested that he join them in a game of cards. With a cheerful smile he agreed.

As the evening and the game progressed, the young man had uncanny good luck in every deal of the cards. The other players all felt that there was something familiar about the handsome young man, as though they had seen him many times before but couldn't place him. Oddly enough, he knew many of them by name, but never introduced himself.

It was nearly morning when another patron entered. As he removed his coat and boots, he called to the innkeeper. "What's happened to your sign? I thought I had the wrong tavern."

The others, surprised, looked out the window to see the swinging sign outside the door. Wiping the steam from the glass, they saw with astonishment that there was nothing upon the sign but the words "Buxton Inn." But the painting of a young cavalier was gone. Then they knew.

With wonder and fright they turned back to the fireplace, but the dapper young card player was gone, leaving nothing but a small puddle of melted snow beneath the chair where his boots had rested. No wonder he had looked familiar.

Almost fearfully they turned again to look at the tavern's sign. Was it a trick of the storm? For now, as clearly as ever, they could see the painting of young Sir Charles in his tall beaver hat and flowing cape, as he had stood for many years. Then something else caught their eye— something they had never noticed before. One of the pockets of his breeches seemed to be bulging as though with many coins, and a smile played about the painted mouth—the kind of smile a young man might wear when he has been lucky at cards.

The Anniversary Party

The young man was out with his girl for a moonlight ride on a backroad in western Massachusetts, when he ran out of gasoline. He left the girl in the car and started walking back down the road for help. When he had gone about a mile or so, he saw a light in the distance and hurried towards it.

The light, he soon found, came from a farmhouse set back from the road by a dirt path. He had driven past the farmhouse a few minutes before, but at that time had seen no light. In fact, he and his girl friend had spoken of how sad the old house had looked with its broken windows, hanging shutters, and collapsed porch steps. Perhaps he had been looking at another house, but it *seemed* to be the same.

He walked up the path and took a closer look. Now he was *sure* it was the same house. But what a difference! It was now ablaze with lights. Sounds of laughter and music drifted down towards him from across the neatly trimmed lawn. As he stood dumbfounded he heard a stamping of horses' hooves. He peered into the side yard and saw about 20 carriages with horses tethered to hitching posts.

That too was strange, for such carriages hadn't been seen in quantities for a half-century. Perhaps, the boy thought, the party was a reunion of horse-and-buggy collectors or something like that. Anyway, he thought, they might have some gas somewhere about, so he walked towards a door on the side porch. On the way, he stopped and looked in a front window. Inside, he saw about 45 New Englanders dressed in the fashions of 1905, eating and drinking and dancing.

The boy glanced at his watch. It was exactly a quarter to twelve. At that moment a piercing scream came from within, the high-pitched shriek of a woman. And at the same instant the lights went out. The boy stood stock-still in terror, unable to move or run.

Seconds later, when his eyes adjusted to the moonlight, he realized with another shock that he was staring through a broken and dirty window into an empty room. The shutters hung crazily, and the windowsill under his hands crumbled with rot. He turned and fled down the path and back up the road.

Later when he told his story to people who knew the area, they told him that just fifty years before, on the anniversary of that night and at a quarter to midnight, a young girl had been murdered in that very room by a jealous lover.

The young man still lives in western Massachusetts and is now in his fifties. Now, however, he carries an extra can of gas in his car.

5. SEA-FARING GHOSTS

The seas are mysterious and strange worlds unto themselves. Many things happen on their shores, upon their surfaces and beneath their waves that are difficult to explain away. The following mysteries of the deep are just a few that have never been solved.

The Tale of the Strangled Figurehead

The Portuguese seamen who tell this weird tale swear it is true.

During the days of the wooden ships and iron men of the last century, a Portuguese sea captain, engaged to a dark-eyed beauty of the Virgin Islands, was determined to have her likeness made into a figurehead for his ship. The girl was flattered by the suggestion until he insisted that she be portrayed wearing her bridal gown. This, she said, would bring bad luck to them both.

The young captain scoffed at her superstition. How could the figurehead bring anything but *good* luck when she was so lovely and the gown so beautiful? Finally, in tears, the bride-to-be consented and posed for the wood carver in her wedding dress. When the figure was shaped and sanded, she agreed that it was a good likeness, even to the bouquet of flowers she held in her hands.

Amid mixed expressions of congratulations and superstitious anxiety from Virgin Islanders, the figurehead was attached to the vessel's prow under the bowsprit. The young captain sailed off on a short voyage that would bring him back just in time for the wedding a few weeks later. The wedding was never to take place.

On the return voyage a dark high-seas storm overtook the vessel. For days it was touch and go as to whether or not she and her captain and crew would survive. Finally the storm blew itself out and the crew scrambled over the rigging to inspect the damage. Much to their dismay they found that a swinging rope had wound itself about the neck of the beautiful figurehead on the prow. They quickly untangled it. They hesitated to tell the young captain of their discovery, but the crew's superstitious rumors soon came to his ears. He too began to worry. Spreading all available sail, he raced for home and his bride-to-be.

A sad-faced group of friends greeted the ship at the dock. A tragedy had taken place, they told the captain, and asked that he hurry to his fiancée's house. There her tearful parents told him that his bride had died the night of the great storm. The grief-stricken man managed to ask how, but almost before they told him, he knew.

She had dressed herself in her wedding gown to have

some minor alterations done by the seamstress. She had hurried up to the attic to fetch a bit of silk lace. On the way down the stairs she had tripped on the long skirt and fallen, catching her long trailing veil on a peg by the stairs. When her parents had found her, she was already dead—strangled by her own wedding veil.

Ghost on the Beach

The Bahamas, vacation islands off the east coast of Florida, have been visited by pirates, phantom ships and ghosts as well as by tourists. Great Isaac, a small cay of the group, about a hundred miles northeast of Miami, was the setting for a very eerie visitation.

In 1810, long before there was any lighthouse on Great Isaac Cay, a great storm left tragedy and wreckage behind it. Several ships sank, and many bodies were washed ashore. One of the bodies was a drowned woman who somehow still clutched a living baby in her arms. Rescuers on the cay quickly removed the baby and in time nursed it back to health.

Years later, when workmen were erecting a lighthouse on Great Isaac, one of them met a hooded woman walking along the beach one night. Her arms were outstretched and she was crying, "My baby, my baby!" over and over again. The workman started to rush to her aid, but then he saw that the rising moon shone right through her figure onto the sand. He stopped in his tracks and rushed back to the camp. Laughter and jeers greeted his story, so from then on he kept it to himself. But not for very long, for he was not alone in meeting the phantom of the beach.

Soon afterwards the foreman of the work crew met the same woman. Then another workman saw her as well. The laughter stopped. When the work crew left, they warned the lighthouse keeper about her. This was in August of 1859.

From that day on, usually after a hurricane or bad storm, and when the moon was rising, the phantom lady was seen and heard walking the beach.

Then in 1913 she appeared in a most unusual way. She attempted to climb the stairs of the lighthouse itself.

The keeper was on his way down when he heard her and saw her coming up the spiral stairs towards him. For a moment he was panic stricken. Then he raced back up the ladder, slammed the trap door behind him and anchored it down with a heavy crate of machine parts. There he stayed until a full hour after dawn before he dared move the crate away and climb downstairs, half expecting to meet her at every turn. He requested a transfer the following day, but it was almost a year before the new keeper arrived. He was of sterner stuff and decided to rid the island of the phantom lady for good.

He gathered several Bahamians together around the light and held a solemn funeral service on the beach where the mother and child had originally been found, to put her tortured soul at rest. From that day on there has been no report of the return of the grieving mother searching for her lost child.

Women All in White

Men who spend much of their lives at sea are full of tales of premonitions and strange apparitions.

Take, for example, the strange dream of the women in white in the rain that plagued John Nelson, the cook aboard the schooner *Sachem*, out of Gloucester. The *Sachem*, under the command of Captain J. Wenzell, had been fishing along Brown's Bank. On September 7, 1871, she pulled her hook and sailed for George's Bank to try for better luck.

That night, as recorded in the log and journal of Captain Wenzell, John Nelson hurried aft to talk to the captain. He was greatly agitated and apparently in mortal fear.

He told the captain that he had just awakened from a dream that he had had twice before in his life—a dream that had been followed both times by shipwreck and tragedy. Nelson had dreamed of women, dressed all in white, standing in the rain as though waiting for their men to come back, perhaps from the sea. The cook then begged the captain to head for port or at least to get away from the dangerous George's Bank noted for storms and reefs.

The captain made little of Nelson's fears and urged him to go back to his galley and prepare the evening meal. Mumbling that it would be fatal to stay there after the warning of the "women all in white," Nelson left.

Later that night it began to blow. About 1:30 one of the men reported in alarm that the *Sachem* was taking in water. Captain Wenzell hurried below and found six inches of water already sloshing in the hold. He quickly ordered that the pumps be manned and a bucket brigade be formed to empty the ship, but, despite their efforts, they could not keep ahead of the in-rushing water. The cook was ordered to provision a lifeboat and be ready to leave if necessary.

Believing that the leak might be on the other side, the captain tacked the schooner in the other direction in an attempt to bring the leak above the waterline. This didn't help. In desperation they signaled another schooner, the *Pescador*. At great risk the ships were brought together and the men of the doomed schooner were taken off. Shortly after, the *Sachem* rolled over on her side and then slid below the waves, bow first. Once more the "women all in white" had been right!

The Mystery of the *Seabird*

On a strip of land near Newport, Rhode Island, there was a little settlement known as Easton's Beach. Only a few farmers and some fishermen and their families made their homes there.

One day in 1880, a fisherman working on his boat near shore suddenly sighted a full-rigged ship of good size heading straight for land. He thought it very odd that such a large ship under full sail should make no attempt to turn away or head along the coast. But it was coming along steadily and directly in the onshore breeze. He called to the other fishermen nearby and ran to the settlement above the beach to alert the rest of the townsfolk.

Soon everyone was on the beach, watching in helpless silence as the strange ship came on as though determined to wreck itself, its canvas straining and flags snapping at the mastheads.

With horror the spectators heard the grating of the hull upon the bottom as it struck. Yet the ship still bore down, keeping straight on course as it cut a keel groove in the sandy ocean bottom. When it finally came to rest, it was still on an even keel, with the bowsprit almost over their heads.

Then they recognized the ship. It was the *Seabird*, a ship that had been under the able command of Captain John Husham. It had been to Honduras, and was expected that very day in nearby Newport. Not a sound came from the decks.

At once the onlookers crowded on board, and the mystery deepened. Coffee still boiled on the galley stove, food for breakfast was on the table, all navigation instruments and charts were in order. Yet there was no trace of the crew, nor any indication of when, why or where they had gone. The only living thing aboard the ship was a mongrel dog shivering on the deck.

The sea had been calm, the breeze fine, and the *Seabird* had been almost exactly on course for Newport. The crew must have left only shortly before the ship appeared on the horizon. But why should they have left the ship when they were so close to their home and families?

Only Heaven and a mongrel dog knew what had happened aboard the *Seabird* that sunny morning.

The Great Wheel of Light

Phantom ships, sea serpents, mysterious sounds and lights can seem ridiculous to those who did not witness them. But to those who encounter such unusual phenomena, they are very real indeed.

So real are they that they are sometimes recorded in ships' logs, set down in the matter-of-fact language of seafaring men. Such an entry was made on June 10, 1909, in the log of the Danish steamship *Bintang*.

As the *Bintang* steamed through the night in the Strait of Malacca, between Sumatra and the Malay Peninsula, the captain was astonished to see what appeared to be a long beam of light under the water. Like the beam of a searchlight, it seemed to be sweeping across the floor of the sea. The beam passed across the sea before him and was followed by another and then another, like the revolving spokes of a wheel, or the searchlight beams you sometimes see following one another across the sky.

Soon, some distance from the ship, there appeared a brighter spot or hub that seemed to be the point from which the beams of light originated. The beams revolved silently as the rotating "wheel" slowly approached the *Bintang*. In the words of the captain, "Long arms issued from a center around which the whole system appeared to rotate."

The great revolving wheel was so huge that only half of it could be seen above the horizon. As it revolved towards the *Bintang*, the crew stared in dumbfounded amazement. The long arms of light could not possibly be a reflection of their own lights, and there was no other ship in sight.

As the great silent revolving wheel of underwater light came nearer, it seemed to sink lower into the water and grow dimmer. Finally it vanished deep beneath the waves and the Strait of Malacca was once more black and empty.

A record of this strange encounter has been published by the prestigious Danish Meteorological Institute, but no one knows what it was the bewildered men saw that night.

Faces in the Sea

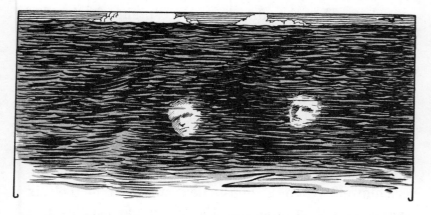

In January of 1925, a huge oil company tanker was plowing through the Pacific towards the Panama Canal when tragedy struck. Two men, overcome by gas while cleaning out an empty cargo hatch, were buried at sea.

Several days later a group of greatly disturbed crewmen approached the captain. They told him an astonishing story. They said that they had seen both the dead seamen following the ship at twilight the past few nights. The captain refused to take their story seriously, but the reports persisted. Even some of the officers saw the apparition.

The heads of the two men would appear in the water off the side of the ship from which they had been buried and would seem to follow the ship for a few moments. Then they would vanish again. Since so many men had seen the apparitions, the captain finally decided to bring the matter to the attention of the officials of the company when they docked in New Orleans.

The company officers listened, at first with disbelief, and then with wonder. One of them suggested that the first mate obtain a camera and be ready for the next appearance of the two ghostly faces in the waves. This was done. Then the officer gave the captain a fresh roll of film with orders to keep it sealed in his own possession until the moment it was to be used. The captain promised to guard the film personally.

Back through the canal went the tanker, and out again into the Pacific. And once more, at twilight, as the ship reached the same spot in the ocean, the two faces appeared alongside.

The captain broke open the film and loaded the camera himself. When the ghosts next appeared, he took six photos and then locked up the camera for safekeeping and away from any possible tampering.

When the ship reached port, the film was taken to a commercial photographer for developing and printing. This man knew nothing about the mystery, nor the reason for the photographs which he processed.

Five of the negatives showed nothing unusual, just waves and spray, but the sixth showed what appeared to be the outlines of two heads and faces in the waves. This photo was enlarged. The two objects showed up plainly, appearing in exactly the same relation to the ship as the two ghosts seen by the crewmen and ship's officers.

These photos eventually were inspected by Dr. Hereward Carrington, a noted investigator of psychic phenomena. He checked the story with company officials, and, after looking at the photo, reported that there could be no doubt that at least one of the faces in the waves was a realistic photo of one of the dead seamen.

Strange things follow the sea, and not all men go down to the sea in ships. Some wear shrouds.

6. GHOST IN THE HOUSE

Why is a house haunted? Why does a ghost need to remain in it, endlessly repeating the same actions? The hauntings in this chapter are of vastly different types, but every one of them reveals the obsession of a troubled spirit. What should be done with a ghost in the house?

The Ghost of Greylock

I can vouch for this ghost-sighting personally. It happened to me.

I once hunted fairly regularly in Massachusetts with a friend named Dick Davis. On one trip, Davis and I decided to work our way up the slopes of Mt. Greylock, in the northwestern corner of the state between Adams and North Adams. Mt. Greylock isn't huge (3,506 feet), but it is rugged, and there were plenty of white-tailed deer browsing on its slopes.

We slept the first night in a haymow and went off separately the next morning. We planned to meet late in the afternoon at a deserted farmhouse we saw up on the slope.

About midafternoon I was hunting along the edge of a swamp when I was startled to hear the shrill blast of a police whistle through the brush. I knew I hadn't passed any red lights, so I waited to see what was coming. It turned out to be an old fellow who lived in the area, who was hunting rabbits with an eager beagle. The whistle was to call the pup. We got to talking and I mentioned meeting Davis at the old farmhouse later. The hunter looked at me sharply.

"Wouldn't go in there, son!" he said. "Better meet your friend out in front."

When I asked him why I shouldn't go into the old house, he mumbled something about "bad flooring," then picked up his shotgun and left with the pup at his heels.

When I got to the farmhouse later, however, I did go in and decided to wait in one of the upstairs rooms. It overlooked an orchard where a few apples might still attract a deer. I settled down to wait. The floors and stairs seemed firm enough to me, even if the old building was run down, long deserted, and had a corner of its roof missing.

About a half-hour after I'd arrived, I heard Dick climb the porch steps, knock snow and mud from his boots, and come in. I decided to keep still and give him a bit of a scare should he start up the stairs. I heard him walking around down below, opening and shutting the old cupboard doors. Then he came to the foot of the stairs just below the room in which I was squatting by the window. He started up and I expected to see his red knitted cap appear over the top step any second. It didn't appear. Perhaps he had seen my muddy tracks and had decided to surprise me, I thought. He was waiting on the stairs. Okay, I'd outwait him.

A half-hour later I was still crouching by the window, waiting. I hadn't heard another sound from the person on the stairs, and by now I was in a rather nervous state, even if I did have a loaded shotgun in my hands. Suddenly a movement in the orchard below caught my eye. It was DICK!

Gun ready, I rose and crept out of the room. The stairs were deserted. I rushed out of the house to meet Dick and never went back in. I've often wondered who or what had started up those old stairs to where I waited, and then changed its mind, for as I hurried out of the house I noticed there were no other tracks but mine on the faded yellow floor.

The Octagon Hauntings

Who is the ghost that resides in the famous Octagon House in Washington, D.C.? Is it the shade of a young suicide? Or the wife of a great president?

The eight-sided brick mansion, built in 1798, stands on the corner of New York Avenue and Eighteenth Street. Now the national headquarters of the American Institute of Architects, it was designed by Dr. William Thornton, who also designed the Capitol. Originally it was built for a Colonel John Taylor of Mount Airy, Virginia. Later President James Madison and his wife Dolley lived there.

The entrance hall of the "Octagon" is circular with curved doors and windows to fit the round walls. Running up to the top of the three-story building from the center of the next hall is a spiral staircase that plays an important part in one story of the Octagon ghost.

The circular entrance foyer extends up through the house, providing a round room on each floor, including the basement. Just outside the basement wall, there is a brick-lined and arched-roof tunnel which comes to a dead end after 20 feet. It is assumed that this tunnel once led to a small creek or bayou along the Potomac River, but no one really knows. . . .

For example, according to another ghost legend—as we shall see—this tunnel may once have led directly to the White House a few blocks away. Through it Dolley Madison is said to have carried valuables, including the famous unfinished Gilbert Stuart painting of George Washington, to keep them safe when the British set fire to the White House in 1814.

According to the first ghost legend, one of Colonel Taylor's 15 daughters ran off and was married against his wishes. When she returned to ask his forgiveness, wearing lilacs in her hair, he said he never wanted to see her again. Without a word she climbed to the top of the great stairwell and with a scream plunged to the lower hall and death. It is said that to this day on rare occasions one can still hear that scream—and the crash of her body to the first floor. On other days, Octagon visitors smell lilacs, another sign that the suicide ghost is close by.

Competing for status with Miss Taylor's shade, of course, is that of Dolley Madison—who, when lilacs are sniffed and screams and crashes are heard, is said to be running through the basement tunnel in panic, in her haste occasionally dropping Washington's portrait with a resounding crash!

The Waterford Ghost's Revenge

It's not often that a ghost has a chance to get revenge on people who are still alive, but near Waterford, New York, supposedly one did just that.

It took place about 1900. At that time, near the end of a barge canal, there lived a carpenter. He was poor and sick with tuberculosis, but he still worked hard to support his wife and two children with earnings from odd jobs about the village.

Unfortunately, his own parents were particularly selfish, cruel and mercenary. They demanded that he will them his house and property, which in case of his death would have gone to his wife. This, of course, the carpenter refused to do. Shortly before he died, however, he warned his parents that if they did anything to harm his family after he was gone, he would come back and haunt them as long as they lived. He would see to it, he said, that they would never make any profit from his house even if they did get it away from his wife.

As soon as their son had passed away, the parents undertook legal proceedings and managed to obtain possession of the property, evicting the impoverished wife and youngsters. The house was run down, but usable, and they hoped to rent it rather quickly. So they closed the blinds and waited for a tenant. But no tenant ever rented it, for presently strange things began to happen.

Some of the neighbors, passing the empty house late at night, noticed lights shining between the shuttered windows and from between loose boards along the sides. At first they thought that perhaps the wife had come back and was living there secretly. They had liked the wife, so they did not investigate too carefully.

However, the lights started to wave about and flicker from within, far too mysteriously for comfort, and people began to cross the road when they passed that way after dark. Rumor spread that the son was making good his promise to keep his parents from making any money from the cottage. As no one wanted to rent the place, it fell more and more into despair. Even in its last years, when it was completely uninhabitable, the mysterious lights could be seen still.

The greedy parents nevertheless kept trying to rent or sell the place. No one would listen to them. The lights continued showing right up until the day when, with a muffled crash and a cloud of dry dust, the sagging roof fell in and the tottering walls collapsed into the cellar hole. Only then did the lights vanish, never to return.

No one could explain the mysterious lights, but many neighbors felt sure that the Waterford ghost had had its revenge.

The Baby Ghost

Tales about baby ghosts are few to begin with, and seldom are they as tragic as this one from upstate New York.

Near the town of Sodus, which is just south of Lake Ontario and about halfway between Rochester and Oswego, there lived a widow and her one-year-old daughter. The recent death of her husband had left the woman somewhat demented. She was extremely nervous and afraid of thunderstorms and lightning.

One night a terrific storm came up from over the lake. The thunder and lightning banged and crashed about her small house for hours. As the storm's fury increased, the poor woman became increasingly panicky. Her baby in its small crib by the fireplace cried louder and louder. Finally the widow's nerves cracked completely and she went mad.

No one knows just what happened, but after the storm was over, a neighbor, who dropped by to see if she was all right, found the woman grovelling on the floor of the little house. The baby was dead in its crib. The neighbors, after examining the small body, decided that the poor woman in a moment of insane rage had killed the child to stop its crying. The mother died a short time afterwards, but for weeks whenever a thunderstorm came up, folks who passed the house claimed they could hear a baby crying inside, although they knew no one was there.

Some months later lightning struck the house and

burned it flat. Only a ruin was left. Still, during thunderstorms, people continued to hear the baby crying above the wind and rain.

Finally, unnerved neighbors banded together to try to stop the cries by completely demolishing the chimney and fireplace. The stones of the chimney were spread about the countryside and all signs of the house were either filled in, covered up, or removed entirely from the site. Then and only then were the plaintive cries of the small child stilled so that folks could walk past the place where the house had been without hearing them.

They say, however, that even today, if the skies are black with an oncoming thunderstorm and lightning crackles across the hills far away, you may still hear a soft and low whimper from the clearing where the house once stood.

The Headless Lady

A Charles Needham, recovering from an illness, rented a small cottage on the edge of the charming town of Canewdon in Southeast Essex, England. The year was 1895 and Needham was settling down to convalesce. The housekeeper/cook he hired for day work seemed concerned that he was planning to sleep in the cottage alone. She kept asking if he thought he would be "all right." He assured her that as far as he knew, he would be, and for two or three nights he was. Then something happened.

He was sitting and reading in the kitchen one midnight, when he was startled by a click of the door latch behind him. The door led to a back-yard garden. He watched the latch lift and then slowly fall again. The door was securely bolted at top and bottom, and whoever it was outside did not try to push against it.

Needham remembered that the front door was unbolted and hurried into the other room. As he slid the bolt home, the latch of that door too began to rise to the top of the slot. It hesitated a moment and then slowly dropped down into place again.

Needham was sick with tuberculosis and not a fit match for an intruder. Nevertheless, he slid back the bolt and threw open the door. There was no one there. For several nights this continued, much to Needham's discomfort, but he decided not to mention the matter either to his housekeeper or to any of the townspeople. He was a lawyer from London and he suspected that youngsters in the neighborhood might be having a little cruel fun with him. He would withstand their pranks, he decided. But a few weeks later he had to change his mind. . . .

He had been visiting a friend in town, a chess-playing doctor, and his host had offered to drive him back to his cottage in his pony cart. They were jogging up to the entrance of the little lane leading to the cottage when suddenly the pony stopped and refused to go farther, in spite of blows from the whip. Needham explained it was only a short walk anyway and got out, thanking his friend for the lift.

As he hurried home, he saw a small light ahead of him along one side of the moonlit road. The trees were thick in that section. Needham assumed the light was a lantern held by another pedestrian on the way home, so he quickened his step to catch up.

A few yards farther on, the figure ahead stepped out into the moonlight, close by his cottage, stood a few moments, and then turned towards him. Needham turned and fled in terror. The figure was a woman, but a woman without a head! Needham ran all the way to the "Chequers," a small inn down the road.

He gave a babbled description of what he had seen, and was amazed to learn that the headless lady was a well-known Canewdon resident who had been murdered and decapitated by her husband many years before. She had once lived in the cottage he had rented. Perhaps she had been trying to enter and set up housekeeping again when she found the doors bolted against her.

Needham slept at the inn that night. The next day, he moved.

The Black Thing in the Cellar

This ghost tale from New Jersey may illustrate the moral that if you happen to have a ghost in your house, the most practical course of action is to be hospitable. It might even pay off in hard cash. . . .

It seems that a house in Trenton had been known to be haunted for many years, and nobody would rent it, in spite of its being an attractive little cottage in a nice neighborhood. Finally a local man with a rather bad reputation appeared and offered to take it over. The owner informed him of the house's reputation and detailed its history. The man was not at all fazed. He laughed and signed the lease, saying he wasn't afraid of man, monster, or ghost.

One night, after living in the house about a week, the tenant had to go into the cellar. He took a candle and headed down. He was two steps above its stone floor when a huge black "thing" rose up at the bottom of the stairs. It had two glowing yellow-white eyes that seemed to stare clear through him. The man was startled but instead of fleeing he swore at the phantom and hurled his candlestick at it.

The neighbors found him a day or so later. He was alive, but all his hair was burned off, and he was a mass of bruises from head to toe. He moved out as soon as he was able to.

The next tenant was a gentle elderly lady who did a great deal of work for the local church. She had heard about the phantom, but the little house was inexpensive and it suited her and she decided to move in, ghost or no ghost. She would take her chances, she said. It was lucky for her that she did.

After several days in the house, with no disturbance, she too had to go to the cellar after dark. As the gleam of the candle lighted up the stone cellar, the black thing rose up before her. She held the candle higher and said very calmly, "My, you startled me, my friend, but what in the name of heaven do you want? Is there anything I can do to help you, as long as we are going to live here together?"

To her astonishment the black shape motioned for the lady to follow. It slowly drifted back across the stone flagging of the floor to an old wooden chest in the corner. She followed with the candle and obeyed the directions of the "thing" when it motioned for her to move the chest aside. It was empty, and she moved it easily. She found a loose flagstone underneath. The murky figure motioned for her to lift the flagstone, and again she complied.

Underneath it was a lead-lined box full of old gold coins. She stared at them for a moment. Then, half to herself, she said, "Can these be for me?" and turned to look at the phantom. It was gone but a cool breeze touched her on the cheek, in an almost friendly caress.

7. SAVED BY A GHOST!

Some ghosts are not much fun, but they are even better—protective spirits who warn the living of danger. They sometimes even actively save lives. Here are a few intriguing tales of their extraordinary helpfulness.

Lord Dufferin's Story

Lord Dufferin, a British diplomat, was the central figure of this story, which has become one of England's classic tales of the supernatural.

One night during a stay at a friend's country house in Ireland, Lord Dufferin was unusually restless and could not sleep. He had an inexplicable feeling of dread, and so, to calm his nerves, he arose and walked across the room to the window.

A full moon illuminated the garden below so that it was almost as bright as morning. Suddenly Lord Dufferin was conscious of a movement in the shadows and a man appeared, carrying a long box on his back. The silent and sinister figure walked slowly across the moonlit yard. As he passed the window from which Lord Dufferin intently watched, he stopped and looked directly into the diplomat's eyes.

Lord Dufferin recoiled, for the face of the man carrying the burden was so ugly that he could not even describe it later. For a moment their eyes met, and then the man moved off into the shadows. The box on his back was clearly seen to be a casket.

The next morning Lord Dufferin asked his host and the other guests about the man in the garden, but no one knew anything about him. They even accused him of having had a nightmare, but he knew better.

Many years later in Paris, when Lord Dufferin was serving as the English ambassador to France, he was about to walk into an elevator on his way to a meeting. For some inexplicable reason he glanced at the elevator operator. With a violent start he recognized the man he had seen carrying the coffin across the moonlit garden. Involuntarily, he stepped back from the elevator and stood there as the door closed and it started up without him.

His agitation was so great that he remained motionless for several minutes. Then a terrific crash startled him. The cable had parted, and the elevator had fallen three floors to the basement. Several passengers were killed in the tragedy and the operator himself died.

Investigation revealed that the operator had been hired for just that day. No one ever found out who he was or where he came from.

The Phantom Stagecoach

Many years ago there was a small Arizona frontier town that was kept alive by a nearby gold mine. The town had once been on the stagecoach route, but when the mine petered out and was abandoned, the stage line was discontinued. Now the little town was almost completely cut off from the rest of the settlements. Only a tiny freight line, run infrequently by a local livery stable owner, remained.

One young boy in the poverty-stricken town was always exploring the nearby hills, hoping to find another mine to bring back the people who had moved away, and also the stagecoach, which he had loved. He had always been there to meet the stagecoach when it came tearing into the little town in a cloud of dust.

The other people in town looked upon the boy's prospecting with amusement, but they did not bother him. In fact, they hoped that he would find a mine and bring back prosperity to the town.

One day the boy left for the hills as usual, with his burro and his lunch, but by nightfall he had not returned. As he had always been back by dark before, his folks became concerned. True, he was self-reliant and used to the rough living of the times and the area, but anything might have happened. Finally, just after midnight, he came home, exhausted but excited. The stagecoach, he said, had come back to town after all.

Then he told this story. He had become separated from his burro back in the hills and after searching for a long time he gave up and started home on foot. It was dark by the time he reached the old coach road to town, and he could hear the howls of wolves in the timber of the foothills close by. He hurried, but the cries of the wolves behind him became louder and louder. In panic he climbed to the top of a high rock by the roadside to wait for the pack to close in.

Just as the wolves approached, he heard the noise of a stagecoach coming along the old road. A dark stage drawn by black horses pulled around the bend and came to a leather-creaking stop beside the rock where he clung in terror. The driver motioned for him to climb in, and then the coach raced towards town with the wolves howling right behind. His parents had trouble believing the boy's story. No one had seen the stagecoach in years and the boy was known to have an active imagination. But the strangest part was to come to light the next day.

Just outside of town a huge grey wolf was found, obviously run over by a heavy wagon or stagecoach. The tracks of the vehicle came right to the edge of town, and then they stopped. They did not turn around and go back—they just stopped, as though they had vanished with the coach that made them. Something had brought the boy back to safety—and it was certainly more substantial than imagination.

The Doctor's Visitor

Dr. S. Weir Mitchell of Philadelphia was one of the nation's foremost neurologists during the latter part of the 19th century. One snowy evening after a particularly hard day he retired early, and was just falling asleep when his doorbell rang loudly. He hoped it had been a trick of his ears, or that his caller would go away, but the bell rang again even more insistently. Struggling awake, he snatched a robe and stumbled down to see who it was. He muttered in annoyance as he slid the bolt to unlock the door, completely unprepared for the shivering child who stood in the swirling snow.

The small pale girl trembled on the doorstep, for a thin frock and a ragged shawl were her only protection against the blustering snow-filled wind. She said in a tiny, plaintive voice, "My mother is very sick—won't you come, please?"

Dr. Mitchell explained that he had retired for the night and suggested that the child call another doctor in the vicinity. But she wouldn't leave, and looking up at him with tear-filled eyes, pleaded again, "Won't *you* come, please?" No one—and certainly no doctor—could refuse this pitiful appeal.

With a resigned sigh, thinking longingly of his warm bed, the physician asked the child to step inside while he dressed and picked up his bag. Then he followed her out into the storm.

In a house several streets away he found a woman desperately sick with pneumonia. He recognized her immediately as someone who had once worked for him as a servant, and he bent over the bed, determined to save her. As he worked, the doctor complimented her on her daughter's fortitude and persistence in getting him there.

The woman stared unbelievingly at the doctor and said in a weak whisper, "That is impossible. My little girl died more than a month ago. Her dress is still hanging in that cupboard over there!"

With strange emotions, Dr. Mitchell strode to the cupboard and opened it. Inside hung the little dress and the tattered shawl that his caller had worn. They were warm and dry and could never have been out in the storm!

The Indian Guide

In the pioneer days of the Old West a family had settled on the edge of a wide forest. Close by in the woods lived an old Indian couple who were very friendly. The old Indians and the little daughter of the pioneer family were particularly fond of each other.

One winter when the youngster was about six she started walking through the woods to visit another little girl who lived in a cabin about a mile away. She had gone there alone many times before; so her parents thought nothing of her making the trip again, even though it was winter and it looked like snow. There were few wild animals in the forest, and no wolves had been seen in the area for many years. A few hours later, when it started getting dark, her parents became concerned. When her father stepped out into the twilight to look for her, he found, to his dismay, that it was snowing heavily. There was no sign of his small daughter.

At once he and his oldest boy bundled up in their heaviest clothes, took a lantern and musket and started off at a trot down the trail to the other cabin. As they ran along they kept calling the little girl's name, but their only reply was the howling of the wind and an occasional hoot from a great grey owl.

At the neighbor's house they learned that the little girl had left some time ago, before the snow began, and should have arrived home long before. Their alarm mounted. But perhaps, they reasoned, she had left the trail to visit the hut of the old Indian couple.

The girl's brother turned off to visit the Indians, while her father and neighbors headed homewards, fanning out through the dark woods to see if they might find the girl before the snow and storm covered up all tracks.

The men reached home first and were overjoyed to find the little girl safe by the fire, drinking hot broth while her mother dried her clothes. She had lost her way, she told them. After stumbling in the drifts for a while, she had started to cry. Almost at once her old Indian friend had appeared and led her home, holding her tiny hand in his all the way, until they could see the lights of her cabin ahead. Then he had smiled at her and vanished into the dark woods behind them.

Her brother returned from the Indians' hut with a sad tale. There, he said, he had found the old squaw huddled by the body of her husband, who had died two days before.

Protection from Beyond

In America's Old West, tomahawks were often the instrument of death for many courageous pioneers. At least once, however, this weapon played an exciting and mysterious part in saving a child from a tragic end.

A hardy settler and his family lived in a cabin far out in the wilderness. Wolves frequently raided the flocks and were even said to attack people when hunger made them ravenous. To add to the dangers, Indians still roamed the area, looking for whatever they could steal. Occasionally they attacked a cabin, burned it and killed the inhabitants.

One day the seven-year-old daughter of the family came upon a very old and sick Indian in the woods. Instead of running away in panic, she helped the ancient man to the cabin and pleaded with her folks to care for him. In spite of their misgivings, her parents agreed. It soon became clear that he did not have long to live.

Although the old man could speak no English, he and the little girl became fast friends. She did everything she could to make his last days comfortable, and he was obviously very grateful. Just before he died he called the girl and her parents to his bedside. Giving his tomahawk to the child, he motioned to the father to hang it on the wall over her small bunk. His wish was granted, although the family could not understand why he insisted on it.

Some weeks later, while the father and mother were away and the little girl was napping in her bunk, a gaunt wolf slipped out of the forest and headed for the cabin. He slunk up to the door, sniffed a few times and then pushed against it. It swung open. He entered the house, his yellow eyes focusing on the tiny girl asleep in the bunk before him.

When the parents returned they were horrified to see a huge wolf apparently crawling into their cabin. They raced across the clearing, shouting, but the wolf did not move. He was dead, his skull crushed from a terrible blow on the head. Their daughter was still asleep in her bunk.

Later, the father jokingly said that perhaps the old Indian had come back to protect the little girl with his tomahawk. Something impelled him to lift the crude weapon from its peg over the bunk. As he looked at it, his laughter ceased.

The blade was splotched with dried blood and in the rawhide thong that bound the primitive blade to the stout handle were several long grey hairs, such as might be found on the head of a timber wolf!

8. BIZARRE!

Almost everyone has experienced some peculiar feeling or event, or heard a fantastic tale from a thoroughly reliable source. And when it happens to you—or to someone you trust—the occurrence is hard to ignore. Even when it is bizarre. . . .

The Ghost with the Flaming Fingers

Every small town along the Hudson Valley in New York State has a pet ghost. Take, for instance, the famous ghost said to have been seen near Leeds, a few miles northwest of Catskill. She was a novel ghost for several reasons.

In the late 1700's, an unpleasant character named Ralph Sutherland came to this country from Scotland, bringing a servant girl with him. He abused the young woman to the point where she could not stand it. At last she ran away.

Sutherland's anger knew no bounds. He mounted his horse and overtook her as she fled down a country road. Then he tied her hands together and, leaping upon his horse, dragged her back to the house. Some said he tied her to the horse's tail. In any case, she was dead when they arrived home.

Sutherland was arrested and tried. He claimed that he had not meant to harm the girl, but only to teach her a lesson. The horse had become frightened and had run away, he said, throwing him and dragging her to her death.

Sutherland's sentence to death was suspended until he should reach 99 years of age, if he lived that long. In the meantime he was to wear a hangman's noose about his neck and report to the judges at Catskill once a year. This, it is reported, he did. But in the meantime the ghost of the young girl began to haunt the area. She was seen sitting on the stone wall of the Sutherland garden with flames rising from each finger tip as she laughed long and loudly at the fear she aroused in the vicinity. At other times she was said to have been seen tied to a black horse's tail as it dragged her shrieking past Sutherland's house night after night.

But here the legend becomes confused. An almost identical account of the ghost of Leeds has the villain's name as Bill Salisbury, and the girl as a native American sent to him as a servant by parents who couldn't control her. Furthermore, Salisbury was supposed to be hanged at 90 instead of 99, and instead of a noose he had to wear a red string about his neck.

This legend has the girl sitting on a rock—Spook Rock, it's called—with a lighted candle on each finger tip instead of flames, and a shaggy white dog howling, heartbroken, at her feet.

The Old Man of the Woods

Presque Isle, Maine, one of the most remote spots in the United States, is perhaps for this reason the setting for many peculiar legends and tales. A resident of Presque Isle reported the following weird incident to me during World War II.

Near where this man's father had lived as a boy, there was a Presque Isle family with two children, a boy and a girl. The youngsters had no friends to play with in the deserted area and so had to invent their own games and entertainment. They often took walks in the nearby woods. One day they began to talk about a nice old man who lived in a cabin back over the hills. At first the parents were concerned, but no one knew of any such man, nor could his cabin be found. They decided he had been dreamed up by the children to make up for their lack of real friends. So they didn't give the matter any thought.

As time went on the children began to report some things the old man said would happen to the local residents, their livestock and crops. Strangely enough, almost all these dire events took place. People lost their crops, their livestock died, and folks were taken sick just as the children's new-found friend had said they would. The parents of the youngsters didn't approve of the morbid interest in death and destruction that their children were displaying. The children were refused permission to visit the woods any more, but they still sneaked away whenever they could.

Finally the parents delivered an ultimatum. Either the children would bring the old man home to meet them or they would be forbidden ever to see him again. The boy and girl said they would invite him, but they were not sure he would come. Off they went into the woods. The parents laughingly waited, assuming there was no such person at all, but marvelling at how the children could have gone off so full of confidence. They soon found out.

A half-hour later the two children returned. A tall bearded man, obviously very old but with a strong, active stride was with them. He was dressed strangely in a suit of black material that had twinkling glints of gold here and there. His battered hat, while old, appeared to be made of some special black fur felt. His beard was pure white and his blue eyes were piercing. He greeted the parents pleasantly, and soon they were reassured that their children had indeed found an interesting and unusual friend.

After staying a while the old man bade them farewell and asked if the children could walk back with him to the edge of the woods to say good-bye. The parents agreed, and off the three started, the man holding the youngsters by their hands. As they walked towards the sunset, the parents were startled to see that only the children cast any shadows. There was none for the bearded man between them.

Neither the old man nor the children were ever seen again.

The Ghost of Dead Man's Curve

In 1908, a local trolley line ran from Port Chester to Rye Village and Rye Beach in New York State. The tracks crossed a road that was simply a right-of-way raised up over a swamp. A hand-operated switch at the crossing point could throw the trolley on either of two routes.

This swampland was full of tall reeds, cattails, pools of dark evil-smelling water and, reputedly, quicksand—a highly unlikely place for human beings to venture. But apparently one unfortunate person did. Or did he?

One late night the trolley rocked and clattered down the tracks to the crossing point. The motorman stopped and got down to throw the switch so that he could proceed towards Rye. There were two passengers in the huge dimly lighted car, one seated at each end. Neither man paid any particular attention to the other.

After the motorman had climbed down to the switch, one of the men also got up and left the car. The switch was thrown. The motorman came back to his post, and the car started along, picking up speed. For some time the remaining passenger did not realize that the other man had not returned. When he did, and told the motorman, they were almost in Rye. The motorman reported the lost traveler, and a search party was quickly organized, for the swamp was known to be treacherous.

But neither that search party nor one formed the next day could find any trace of the missing man. Where could he have gone?

The most logical explanation was that the man, probably a stranger, had set off across the swamps and had perished in one of the bottomless pools or in quicksand. Nothing, certainly, was ever seen or heard of him again.

From then on, until the trolley line was discontinued, that crossing point in the swamp was known as "Dead Man's Curve" and people gave it a wide berth on dark nights or gloomy days. Those who did occasionally walk along the tracks often reported low moans or faint calls for help, whistling, and splashing from deep in the marshland.

Perhaps they were the natural voices of the swamp, the calls of birds, or the moaning of the wind in the bulrushes . . . or perhaps they were the regretful cries of the shade of an ill-fated traveller, who stepped out of a trolley and into eternity.

The Haunted Schoolhouse

The small schoolhouse in Newburyport, Massachusetts, was the scene of a strange phenomenon in 1870. Every day a mysterious yellow glow spread over the classroom, windows, and blackboards. It usually started near the hall door and spread silently over the room. After about two minutes it faded away. It did no harm while it cast its light over the room, but afterwards the students and the teacher, Miss Lucy A. Perkins, felt weak and ill.

The yellow radiance was not the only unusual occurrence. There was also a gust of cold air that swept through the room, even when the doors and windows were tightly closed. The chill breeze rustled the papers, swung the faded map on the wall and shook the hanging lamp. This too, made the teacher and children feel slightly ill, but Miss Perkins kept the class going day after day, trying bravely to ignore the strange event.

In the late fall the yellow light disappeared and a low-pitched laugh was heard. The eerie sound echoed in the tiny attic, the small coal cellar and the hall. One day many of the students, and Miss Perkins, saw a child's hand floating in the air. Then the arm became visible. The climax came on November 1.

During a geography lesson, Miss Perkins called upon a student to recite. In the midst of a sentence he suddenly stopped and pointed to the hall. There stood a boy with his arm upraised. It was the same arm and hand that had floated in the air.

The boy stood silently, his face bound in a white cloth as though he had an injured jaw or a toothache. Then, as they watched, he slowly vanished. From that time on, the schoolhouse was plagued no more.

The authorities questioned three local boys who had a reputation for mischief in an attempt to solve the mystery, but decided they had had no part in the events. To this day the yellow glow, the cold breeze and the boy with the upraised arm and bandaged jaw have never been explained.

9. VANISHED!

There is something frightening about the sudden disappearance of people or things. This is particularly true when there is no way to explain it. One moment they are there and the next they have vanished without a trace. There are tales of vanishing individuals, ships, planes—even whole towns. Here are a few of the most baffling.

The Man Who Fell Forever

"Curly" was a sailor who was fascinated by high places. No mast was too tall for him to climb, no cliff too sheer for him to peer over and no tower too shaky for him to explore. He frequently talked of what a wonderful sensation it must be to fall from a great height.

When his ship dropped anchor at a South American port, Curly was determined to climb an old abandoned stone lighthouse. His friends argued that he couldn't get to the top, and placed bets on him. Another sailor went along with Curly to act as a witness. And so the two entered the musty, damp old tower and started up the crumbling stone stairway.

At last they emerged on a balcony far above the sand dunes. But when they tried to attract the attention of their friends, who were playing cards directly beneath them, their shouts did not carry. Finally, Curly's companion tied his jackknife in his handkerchief, Curly added his lucky coin for weight, and they tossed the little bundle over the rusty iron railing. They lost sight of it as it fell to the depths below, but still did not attract the attention of the other men. Annoyed, they decided to start back down. Curly hesitated a moment. Then with an odd grin he said, "I know a quicker way!" and hurled himself over the old railing, plummeting directly down toward the group below.

The other man screamed a warning and then bounded down the stairs, frantic at the thought of what he would find when he reached the bottom. He burst out the old doorway, hoping that nobody else had been hurt by Curly's leap. To his astonishment, the rest of the group was still playing cards, as though nothing had hurtled down upon them from the tower above. Nothing had. Curly hadn't landed!

The group searched the ground for yards around, combing the tower, the dunes and the water below them, but Curly wasn't there. He was never seen again. They did find the tied and knotted handkerchief containing the jackknife, but Curly's lucky coin was no longer with it. That too, like Curly, had vanished on the way down.

The Man They Couldn't Bury

No one seems to know much about the origin of this tale, except that it happened "way out West" and "way back when." The setting was in a rough-and-ready cattle-raising area where law and its enforcement were often swift and abrupt, though not always accurate. Hangings by lynch mobs were common. They were the almost inevitable punishment for cattle and horse thieves, crop burners, and mine-claim jumpers.

For several months before this incident took place cattle had been disappearing from the local herds. Suspicion finally fell upon an old codger who lived alone up a canyon a few miles outside of town. He didn't have any cattle, nor could people figure out what he had done with them, but they suspected him all the same. The case against him was simply that no one else was available to blame.

Small groups of men gathered in the saloons and talked about what could be done to stop the thefts. Some of them insisted that they couldn't take justice into their own hands without some proof that the old man *had* taken the cattle. At least, they might try catching him in the act. Others held that they had to hang *somebody* for the crime.

As the cattle continued to vanish, feelings grew hotter until one day the mob got completely out of hand and headed for the little hut where the old man lived. They found it empty, but as they were leaving, up strolled the old chap leading his horse. A fresh cowhide was tied to his saddle. There, apparently, was evidence enough that he had been killing cows and skinning them for their hides. This would explain why people had never been able to find any live cattle about his canyon or any other signs that he had been stealing them.

The old codger stoutly maintained his innocence. He said that he had found a single dead cow and had skinned it because it had not had a brand on it. The mob examined the hide and, sure enough, could find no brand. But a section of the cow was missing—that part where a brand might easily have been located. This was proof enough for the mob, and they hurried the old man down the mountain to the small town.

In order to make this a spectacle for the instruction of other possible cattle thieves, they decided to erect a scaffolding and hang him in style, instead of just throwing a rope over a convenient tree. The old chap maintained that even if they did hang him they'd never bury him as a cattle thief, and swore long and loud to that effect while they hammered the scaffold together in the town square.

When all was ready and the crowd waiting, the gang leader sprang the trap. The old man had spoken the truth. He fell through the trap opening but never was actually hung. The empty noose swung crazily in the air—for the victim had vanished. A cold gust of air whipped over the crowd about the scaffold. Neither the old man nor the missing cattle were ever seen again.

Tragedy Atop the Glacier

In this day of flights over long stretches of water, uncharted jungles and polar wastes it is small wonder that occasionally an aircraft and its passengers are lost forever. Usually some evidence is recovered to settle the fate of the passengers, but sometimes the tragedy has an unexplained and bewildering twist.

The Curtiss C-46 "Commando," sometimes referred to as "Dumbo," was a huge aircraft with two engines, but it could carry on with one if necessary. It had two floors, the upper for passengers and the lower for baggage, cargo or extra fuel in special tanks. It was a rugged ship and it took many men and supplies to their destination safely and quickly during the Second World War.

One of those efficient C-46's carried 32 men, most of them members of the military services, on a flight over the state of Washington. Although the weather was bad, the flight was routine. After the plane passed a mountainous section of the state southeast of Seattle, where Mount Rainier flaunts its 14,408 feet of grandeur, it was not heard from again.

There was complete silence.

A state-wide search was begun for the missing craft. Planes spotted a smudge high on one of the glaciers, at the 11,000-foot level. Closer inspection revealed bits of metal, wings and the remains of fire. A ground rescue party set off for the spot.

Backbreaking hours later the searchers reached the spot on Tahoma Glacier where the wreckage had been seen. There lay the crumpled transport in scattered bits and broken metal parts. Bloody bulkheads gave mute testimony to the terrific crash against the icy slope in the blinding storm.

The rescue party started a thorough search for bodies—hoping that perhaps by some miracle a few men might still be alive. They looked among the broken parts, into the hollows in the glacier and under crazily tilted wing scraps and cabin wreckage. Then they began to realize that this was no ordinary plane crash. Not only were there were no survivors from the crash, there were no bodies—or traces of them—living or dead! In spite of the evidence that the plane had been carrying 32 men when it crashed, not one body was found—ever. Where did the 32 men go, how did they vanish and why?

Eskimo Village

Strange things have happened in the long winters of the Far North, but none more baffling than what occurred to an Eskimo village in 1930.

A French-Canadian trapper named Joe LaBelle planned to visit friends at a remote Eskimo village on the shores of Lake Angikuni. As he drew near the village, he noticed that the usual bedlam of the sled dogs was missing. That was odd, he thought, as he approached the little cluster of low sod huts and crude tents spread along the frozen lake shore. Near the first hut he called a greeting, but no answer came.

He lifted the flap of skin over the doorway on one of the hunts and peered inside. It was empty and showed signs of having been abandoned in great haste. He went from hut to hut. All were deserted and all bore the signs of frantic departure. Pots were still full of food. Sewing needles of ivory were left in garments. Even the rifles, so necessary to the Eskimos in this Northern wilderness, were abandoned along with food, clothing and personal belongings of all sorts. More than 30 people—men, women, old folks and infants—had vanished.

On the shore of the lake Joe LaBelle found three kayaks, including that of the leader of the village, battered by the winds and waves. Seven sled dogs, starved to death, lay by some tree stumps. An Eskimo grave was open and empty. This was the strangest discovery of all, for opening a grave was unheard of among the Eskimos. And to add to the mystery, the stones that had covered it had been removed and neatly piled in two groups beside the open grave. Certainly this could not have been the work of animals or vandals.

Joe LaBelle hurried to the nearest town to report his discovery to the Canadian Mounted Police. They returned with him to the deserted village and confirmed his story—all the inhabitants had disappeared into the frozen wasteland without a trace, leaving behind the sled dogs and rifles that would have given them their only chance of survival.

Where did the Eskimos go and why? To this day nobody knows.

10. TALES OF TERROR

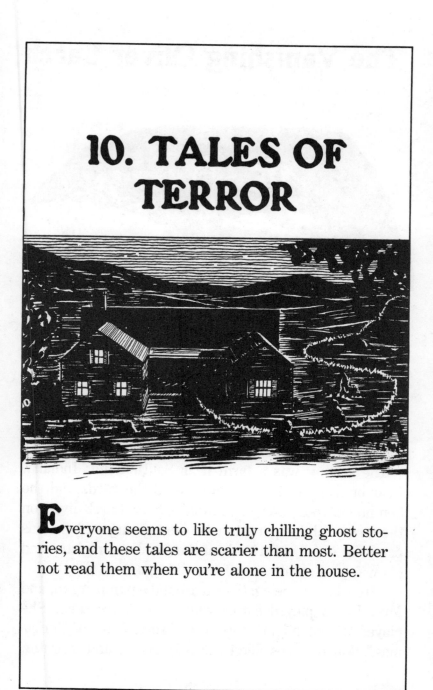

Everyone seems to like truly chilling ghost stories, and these tales are scarier than most. Better not read them when you're alone in the house.

The Vanishing Oliver Larch

It happened in 1889 on Christmas Eve.

The setting was a farm near South Bend, Indiana. Four or five inches of snow covered the yards and the hen-house roof. Eleven-year-old Oliver Larch lived on the farm with his parents who were giving a Christmas party for some old friends of the family, a minister and his wife and an attorney from Chicago.

After dinner they gathered around a pump organ, and Mrs. Larch played carols while the others sang. She played "Silent Night" and "The Twelve Days of Christmas." Warm voices filled the cozy room, and laughter.

After a while Oliver went to the kitchen to pop corn on the wood-burning range.

At this point his father noticed that the gray granite bucket used for drinking water was almost empty. He asked Oliver to run out to the well in the yard and refill it. The boy set aside his corn-popper and put on his overshoes. He picked up the bucket and opened the door to the yard. It was just a few minutes before 11 o'clock. It would soon be Christmas, and he wanted to get back to the party quickly.

His father returned to the living room to add his voice to the chorale, as Oliver stepped out into the night—and eternity. About a dozen seconds after he had left the doorway the adults around the organ were stunned by screams from the yard.

They rushed out the same door Oliver had used. Mrs. Larch grabbed up a kerosene lamp to light the way. Outside, the dark, starless night was filled with scream after scream of, "Help! Help! They've got me! They've got me!"

What made the adults recoil in horror was that Oliver's screams were coming from high *above* them in the blackened sky. The piercing cries grew fainter and fainter and finally faded away completely as the stunned group stared at each other in speechless disbelief.

The men sprang to life, seized the lamp, and followed the youngster's tracks towards the well. They did not get far. Halfway to the well, roughly 30 feet (9 m) from the house; the tracks abruptly ended. No signs of a scuffle or struggle, just the end of the tracks. They found the heavy stone bucket about 15 feet (5 m) to the left of the end of the tracks, dropped in the snow as though from above. That was all. Oliver had started straight for the well, and then had been carried away by—what? He was a big boy, weighing about 75 pounds (34 kg), too heavy for a large bird or even several birds to lift. Airplanes had not been invented yet, and no balloons were aloft that night. Who or what seized Oliver Larch? The mystery has not been solved to this day, and probably never will be.

The Terrible Hand

In 1917 a Mrs. Roy Jackson, now of Harrison, New York, went to live in Paterson, New Jersey with her young husband. They were poor but eventually stumbled on an extremely inexpensive house, even for those days. Mrs. Jackson felt uneasy about the house and at first wanted no part of it, even at $12 a month.

Still, the Jacksons moved in. Even her brother, a lawyer who checked the lease, remarked on the house's vaguely sinister atmosphere. He said he felt a "presence" there that was "not good," but the rent was low.

The months went by and Mrs. Jackson's apprehension grew. Then one day she learned from neighbors that the reason the house was so cheap was that it was supposed to be haunted. A mother had killed herself and two children in the house several years before and since then no one had stayed there longer than a few days. There were rumors of lone women renting the place and being found dead a day later after shrieking, "Someone has me by the throat."

Roy Jackson scoffed at these yarns and insisted they stay on, in spite of his wife's feeling that she was constantly being peered at, followed, and warned to move. Then came the First World War, and Roy began to talk of enlisting. It was on an October night that the young wife came face to face with terror and almost lost her life.

She was lying on a sofa in the living room, thinking

about the changes the war would make in her life and looking at a bright spot on the ceiling—a reflection from the gas fixture on the table. Suddenly she was aware of a second bright spot on the ceiling. Perhaps light from outside? A reflection from a mirror? But there was no other light or mirror.

The spot grew and grew, writhing like "thousands of cobwebs turning and twisting into a mass about three feet long and two feet wide," she said later. A point protruded from the whirling mass, then another and another until she recognized it as a hand with five long pointed fingers. Suddenly the mass stopped whirling.

The mass then grew a long wispy arm behind the fingers, and the entire shape darted down from the ceiling, seizing Mrs. Jackson by the throat. With an agonized lurch, she hurled herself to the floor and lay on the rug, face down and gasping for breath. Moments later she forced herself out of the room to the stairs. Shaken but unhurt, she finally convinced her husband they should move. One encounter with the grey whirling terror had been enough.

Out of curiosity the Jacksons returned to Paterson in 1930 and visited their ex-landlady. She was in great pain from an old injury. It seems that after the Jacksons had left, the house had been rented to a single woman. One night the landlady heard screaming and had run up to help. The spinster lay face down on the floor, dying, but grabbed the landlady in her terror, tearing ligaments that had never healed.

Mrs. Jackson, who recalls her experience vividly, has not recorded the Paterson house number, only that it stood on North Third Street.

The Whistle

On a small isolated farm in South Carolina an old woman lived alone with her dog. One night, as she was going about her chores, she became aware of an odd whistling sound somewhere outside. It did not sound like high wind in the pines, noises of nature, or a human whistle. It was very strange. Curious, she went to the farmhouse door. As she did, she noticed that her small terrier was barking and howling on the back porch. This porch, which was enclosed, made a dark and snug haven for the pup.

She opened the door. The wavering and high-pitched whistle seemed to be coming towards the house from across the hills, yet it was as hard to locate as the chirp of a cricket. It must be some of the local youngsters trying to frighten her, she thought, but she shut and bolted the door and hastily got her late husband's revolver—just in case. She returned to the door to await whatever might be going to happen next. She left the dog on the back porch. If it were just pranksters his barking would frighten them away.

The whistle came nearer, although the old woman could see nothing. Then it seemed to turn, pass slowly around the house and approach the porch, where the now hysterical terrier was almost beside himself with excitement.

Soon there was a terrific outcry and sounds of struggle on the back porch. Then silence—as complete as it was terrifying. The lady, alone in the stillness, shook with fright. She did not dare go out onto the porch. Eventually she went to bed.

The next morning she investigated. The dog was gone, and blood was spattered all about. What had taken place? The whistle had stopped when the struggle began. But what was it that had caused the bloodshed? What had happened to the little terrier? Nobody ever found out.

The Strange Death of Mrs. Reeser

Fire, a great blessing from the days of the cave man on, occasionally sets off mysteries that are as difficult to believe as they are to solve. This was the case in the 1951 death by burning of Mrs. Mary Reeser of St. Petersburg, Florida.

This elderly lady lived alone and was last seen alive by a friend the night before her unusual death. Her friend went to call on her again at about eight o'clock on the morning of July 2, 1951, to take her some coffee and a telegram. To her astonishment she found the handle of the door too hot to hold. In alarm she ran for help. Some carpenters who were working nearby returned with her and forced open the door to Mrs. Reeser's room.

The room was almost unbearably hot although the windows were open. A ghastly sight greeted them. Close to one of the open windows were the charred remains of a chair—and of Mrs. Reeser herself. All that was left of either was a small pile of blackened wood and a skull. A pile of charred wood on the floor contained several coil springs and a few bits of bone.

Nearby another small pile of charred wood marked where a small end table had stood, and a burned floor lamp lay some distance away. The room itself was strangely affected by the fire. Above a line three or four feet from the floor, the walls and curtains were heavily coated with black soot, as were the screens of the open windows.

A base plug in the wall had melted, short-circuiting a lamp and clock which had stopped at 4:20. A small wall-type gas heater was turned off and unaffected by the fire. There had been such terrific heat in the room that candles on another table had melted and run out of their holders onto the table itself. Under the pile of charred wood and bones there was a burned spot on the rug. But nothing else had caught fire.

What happened in that room may never be known. Neither arson experts from the police department and Board of Fire Underwriters, nor doctors could determine what had caused such terrific heat and such strange reactions to it. It was estimated that temperatures up to 3,000° F (1650° C) would be required for such complete destruction of a body and a chair, and not even a burning body, clothing, and wood could generate that temperature, even for a short time.

There had been no lightning that night. Experts determined that no explosive fluids or inflammable chemicals had been present that could raise the ordinary temperature of a fire (such as a cigarette-started fire) to the degree at which such complete cremation could take place. A mirror on the wall was cracked and distant candles melted. Why hadn't other things in the room caught fire? Why wasn't the house destroyed as it would have been in an ordinary fire? Why did it stay so unbearably hot in that room until eight in the morning, even with the windows open?

This was no ordinary fire and no ordinary event. But what was it?

Acknowledgments

It would be impossible for me to name and thank individually all those who have contributed in one way or another to this book. Many of the stories came from total strangers I met casually while tracking down others on the list. Some were sent to me anonymously by readers of my column, others came from long-forgotten diaries, family and town histories. Some were told to me by friends and neighbors who wish to remain nameless.

To all of these people, as well as to the very few ghosts that I have met myself (I think), my deep appreciation.

The hunt has been a long and exciting one, and often in odd places, but the "trophies of the chase" on the preceding pages have made it mighty well worthwhile. I hope you have as much fun reading these stories as I, strangely enough, had tracking them down.

Index